Amir Laurent: Fowl Play a Cuckoo Book 2 Greenhouse Fight

Amir Laurent: Fowl Play a Cuckoo Tale, Volume 2

Maxwell Hoffman

Published by Maxwell Hoffman, 2024.

This is a work of fiction. Similarities to real people, places, or events are entirely coincidental.

AMIR LAURENT: FOWL PLAY A CUCKOO BOOK 2 GREENHOUSE FIGHT

First edition. November 16, 2024.

Copyright © 2024 Maxwell Hoffman.

ISBN: 979-8230761631

Written by Maxwell Hoffman.

Also by Maxwell Hoffman

Acorn Man Savior of the Forest
Acorn Man Savior of the Forest

Amir Laurent: Fowl Play a Cuckoo Tale
Amir Laurent: Fowl Play A Cuckoo Tale Book 1 Opal's Deception
Amir Laurent: Fowl Play a Cuckoo Book 2 Greenhouse Fight

Arctic Shadows: A Lenin Aslanov Story
Arctic Shadows: A Lenin Aslanov Story Book 1: The Finnish Incursion
Arctic Shadows: A Lenin Aslanov Story Book 2 Dmitry's Temper
Arctic Shadows: A Lenin Aslanov Story Book 3 Journey to Iceland

Baron Floofnose: A Capybara's Quest
Baron Floofnose: A Capybara's Quest Omnibus Trilogy

Bellamy's Blunders: Adjusting to Society

Bellamy's Blunders: Adjusting to Society Omnibus Trilogy

Benny Dubious Playbook Scheme Series 3
Benny Dubious Playbook Scheme Trouble in Georgia Book 2: "Moshie's" Fall
Benny Dubious Playbook Scheme Trouble in Georgia Book 3: Hugo's Revelation

Benny Dubiuos Playbook Scheme Nevada Shuffle
Benny Dubious Playbook Scheme: Nevada Shuffle

Frozen Dawn: A Neanderthal's Redemption
Frozen Dawn: A Neanderthal's Redemption Omnibus Trilogy

Ivan Zhuk: Zhuk's Gambit
Ivan Zhuk: Zhuk's Gambit Book 1 Mental Agony
Ivan Zhuk: Zhuk's Gambit Book 2 The MMA Fighter
Ivan Zhuk: Zhuk's Gambit Book 3 Ivan's Freedom

Knox Sovereign: The Juche Wars
Knox Sovereign: The Juche Wars Book 1 Unmasking Knox Sovereign
Knox Sovereign: The Juche Wars Book 2 A Daring Rescue
Knox Sovereign: The Juche Wars Book 3 Fall of Colonel Rex MacManners

Misadventures of Wolfgang Wirrarr
Misadventures of Wolfgang Wirrarr Omnibus Trilogy

Rowan Sunfire Frosty Fugitive Series
Rowan Sunfire Frosty Fugitive Book 3 Defense of Vos Tower
Rowan Sunfire Frosty Fugitive Omnibus Trilogy

Viral Revelations: Ra-E's Visions
Viral Revelations: Ra-E's Visions Omnibus Trilogy

Wiccan Guardian
Wiccan Guardian Omnibus Trilogy

Watch for more at https://www.instagram.com/vader7800/.

Table of Contents

Amir Laurent: Fowl Play a Cuckoo Book 2 Greenhouse Fight (Amir Laurent: Fowl Play a Cuckoo Tale, #2) 1
Part One 3
Prologue 4
Chapter One 12
Chapter Two 20
Chapter Three 28
Part Two 36
Chapter Four 37
Chapter Five 46
Chapter Six 55
Chapter Seven 63
Part Three 71
Chapter Eight 72
Chapter Nine 79
Chapter Ten 86
Epilogue 94

AMIR LAURENT: FOWL PLAY A CUCKOO TALE BOOK 2
GREENHOUSE FIGHT
by
Maxwell Hoffman

2

Part One

Prologue

Amir Surprised

Amir Laurent was surprised to see Catholic priest Arthur Boucher and Islamic preacher Bachir Muhamed greeting him in the living room. His mother Saliha was worried about her son's behavior being to concentrated on the bird known as Opal.

"SON, YOU ARE TOO CONCENTRATED on taking care of that bird instead of yourself" said Saliha, "these two gentlemen are here to help you."

"YOUR BROTHER TAHAR mentioned to me the other day that the bird has practically taken over your life" added Arthur.

TAHAR THOUGHT AMIR, this is all his fault! He will take him away from his beloved Opal!

"I WILL NEVER LET YOU separate me and Opal!" continued Amir.

AMIR WAS BEING DEFIANT, being protective of the bird in question. Arthur and Bachir soon agreed with Tahar's sentiment that the bird was somehow very unnatural. It wasn't even a normal cuckoo bird as both men had speculated it.

"MAY WE SEE THE BIRD for ourselves?" asked Arthur.

AMIR WAS RELUCTANT to show both of them, knowing very well either one of them can just take Opal out of the apartment. He darted right back into the hallway and shut the door to his room.

Back with Opal

AMIR GAZED AT OPAL on her pillow, she was the size of a domestic cat.

"I AM SORRY FOR NOT bringing your food but there are two gentlemen outside willing to take you away from me!" cried Amir.

OPAL COULD TELL THIS was serious, her plan was working after all. Driving the human insane so that he would leave his room and she could dominate the rest of the apartment eventually.

"CHIRP, CHIRP" SAID Opal as she still wanted to sound more like a bird than using her actual language.

"YES, I WILL DO MY VERY best to keep those mean men away from you" said Amir.

TAHAR SOON WOKE UP from the commotion along with Farida. Farida was surprised that her brother Amir was acting so weird.

"WHAT'S GOING ON BROTHER?" asked Farida as she opened her door.

"IT'S AMIR, HE'S GONE insane" continued Tahar.

TAHAR HEADED OVER TOWARDS Amir's door and began to knock on it. KNOCK, KNOCK, KNOCK.

"COME ON AMIR, DON'T play around, Arthur and Bachir just want to help you" said Tahar.

"YOU PUT THEM UP TO THIS!" bellowed Amir.

AMIR WAS MOVING VARIOUS objects in his room to block the door so that it wouldn't open on the other end.

Creating a Barricade

AMIR WAS DOING HIS best being the "father" of Opal, trying to protect her. She was encouraging it all the way with her chirping calls.

"CHIRP, CHIRP, CHIRP!" cried Opal with excitement.

"YES, YES, I AM TRYING to protect you I am sorry I haven't fed you yet because of all of this commotion" continued Amir.

OUTSIDE THE DOOR, TAHAR knew he had to probably call the police to the apartment to get Amir to cooperate. Kamel woke up to see Tahar and Farida glaring at Amir's locked door.

"WHAT'S ALL OF THE RACKET?!" cried Kamel.

"YOUR SO-CALLED RESPONSIBLE son cares too much for that blasted bird" said Tahar.

KAMEL ROLLED HIS EYES and headed towards the door and began to bang on it. BANG, BANG, BANG.

"SON, THIS IS GETTING ridiculous, you open up this door immediately!" bellowed Kamel.

KAMEL AND SALIHA BOTH ran the household, he was trying to get some sense into his son's madness. Saliha, along with Arthur and Bachir headed down the hallway. Saliha gasped how her son had locked himself inside his own room.

"WE HAVE TO CALL THE police, we have no other choice" said Saliha.

KAMEL SIGHED IN AGREEMENT.

An Unusual Call

KAMEL DECIDED TO MAKE the phone call to the police, the operator on the other line felt it was quite odd for what Kamel had to say.

"YES, CAN I HELP YOU?" asked the operator.

"PLEASE GET ME THE POLICE" said Kamel, "my son has locked himself in his room."

"IS HE GOING TO INFLICT harm on himself?" asked the operator.

"NO, BUT HE REFUSES to come out" continued Kamel.

"I WILL DISPATCH AT least two officers to your address" said the operator.

"YES, YES THANK YOU" said Kamel.

KAMEL WAITED PATIENTLY along with the rest of the household. They had anticipated this would be a rather long morning, and perhaps a longer day. For Amir he was trying to find a way out of the apartment altogether. Even though climbing out of the ladder escape route meant for fire escapes.

"I HAVE TO SEE IF I can just get out and take you with me" said Amir.

OPAL WAS AMAZED BY Amir's loyalty to her, she didn't expect things would take this drastic turn so fast. Amir gazed out of the window, he could see a police car approaching the apartment. He knew he would have to figure out something fast.

Chapter One

Police Showing Up Below

Amir couldn't just escape the apartment complex using the fire escape just yet. He could see a police car pulling up to the apartment. Out of the police car came Officers Anna Bessette and Dylan Desmarais. They heard of the unusual report of a cuckoo causing commotion at the apartment.

"THIS IS IT" SAID OFFICER Anna as she looked up.

"YES, TIME TO HEAD IN" said Officer Dylan.

AMIR WAS SPOOKED AS he saw the two police officers heading inside. It would be only a matter of time before they'd show up in his front door. He began to search around trying to figure a way out to take Opal with him.

"DON'T WORRY LITTLE bird, I will try my best to save you" said Amir.

OPAL GAZED AT AMIR on her pillow, she laughed to herself knowing how insane she was driving Amir. Outside the apartment officers Anna and Dylan arrived. Saliha answered the door.

"WE RECEIVED A CALL about a bird causing commotion?" asked Officer Anna.

"YES, THIS WAY OFFICERS" said Saliha.

SALIHA EXPLAINED HOW her son Amir barricaded himself in his room, refusing to come out. The police officers would have to do their best to get him out.

Trying to Talk to Amir

OFFICERS ANNA AND DYLAN met the entire family - Tahar, Farida and Kamel. They soon met Arthur Boucher and Bachir Muhamed - the two religious figures who are family friends.

"WE ARE SO GLAD YOU came, there is no way of getting my son out" said Kamel.

"I SUSPECT THE BIRD he is caring for is a nefarious cuckoo bird" said Tahar, "it's demonic in nature as it's a brood parasite."

"A CUCKOO BIRD YOU SAY?" asked Officer Dylan, "Well, let's see if we can talk some sense in your brother."

SOON OFFICERS ANNA and Dylan approached the door and began to knock on it pretty hard - KNOCK, KNOCK, KNOCK. Those knocks sent shivers down Amir's spine. These were not the normal knocks from his family.

"WHO ARE YOU PEOPLE?!" cried Amir.

"WE ARE POLICE OFFICERS, we'd like to speak to you" said Officer Dylan.

AMIR REFUSED TO ANSWER knowing that he didn't have a lawyer with him at all.

"PLEASE, PLEASE KEEP me safe" said Opal as she was using some sort of mind reading message to Amir.

AMIR FELT HE WAS GOING crazy did the bird just try to speak to him?

Stir Crazy Amir

AMIR STILL DIDN'T KNOW what to do as he marched back and forth in his room. An hour had already passed and the police officers were running out of ideas along with the rest of the family.

"HEY, I GOT AN IDEA why not call in your SWAT team that'd teach him a lesson" laughed Kamel.

"KAMEL, YOU KNOW THIS isn't the right situation to do that" said Saliha.

SALIHA WAS INSULTED by her husband's remarks.

"WELL, A SWAT TEAM WOULD get him to cooperate more with us, but it's a waste of resources" added Officer Dylan.

"I AGREE, BUT HE CAN'T be in his room forever" added Officer Anna.

TAHAR KNEW THIS WAS his fault inviting the two religious friends over hoping to intervene against Amir's behavior. It only made matters worse.

"THIS HAS TO BE MY FAULT, maybe I should speak to him myself?" asked Tahar.

"HEY, WORTH A SHOT WE'LL back you up if anything goes wrong" added Officer Dylan.

TAHAR SIGHED AS HE approached Amir's door and knocked on it.

"AMIR, PLEASE IT'S ME Tahar I am sorry for the trouble I have caused but everyone would like for you to come out" said Tahar.

AMIR REFUSED TO RESPOND feeling it was a trick.

Stubborn Amir

AMIR WAS PROTECTIVE of his pet bird - Opal having raising it since she hatched.

"YOU WILL NEVER GET ME TO COME OUT, I WILL STAY HERE FOREVER!" laughed Amir.

EVERYONE OUTSIDE HIS door were quite shocked by his behavior. Even Saliha soon began to lean in favor of a SWAT team trying to get her son out.

"YEA, I THINK A SWAT team is now called for" said Saliha, "my son isn't a violent person he's just being stubborn with that bird of his."

"SIGH, I HATE TO MISUSE resources like this but we have no choice" said Officer Anna.

OFFICER ANNA MADE THE call to the police station they worked at. The clerk at the dispatch operating area soon began to send the signal to the SWAT team leader.

"WE GOT A CALL OF SOMEONE barricading himself in his room!" said the SWAT team leader.

THE SWAT TEAM LEADER then instructed his colleagues to get ready and they all began to head off. The SWAT van was fully armored heading straight for the apartment complex where Amir lived. This was quite serious the SWAT team leader could tell he heard of a bird also being kept as a strange pet.

Chapter Two

SWAT Team Arrives

The SWAT team soon arrived near the police officers' car and soon they began to head up towards the floor where Amir's room was. The clerk at the front counter was surprised to see the commotion going on.

"SO WE GOT SOMEONE DANGEROUS up there?" asked the clerk.

"ACTUALLY IT'S SOMEONE gone crazy over a bird" added a SWAT team member.

THAT'S ALL THE INFORMATION the SWAT team had on someone like Amir. They knew Amir wasn't the type to do this - the cuckoo had to be influencing Amir's behavior in some form or fashion for this to happen. As they arrived at the front door - Tahar was the one who answered it this time.

"THANK GOODNESS YOU arrived my brother is trapped within his room he barricaded himself" said Tahar.

"DON'T WORRY WE'LL GET him out safely" said the SWAT team leader.

OFFICERS ANNA AND DYLAN stood back with the rest of the family as the SWAT team soon headed down the hallway towards Amir's room. Amir could see flashlights as he looked underneath his door and men with boots he didn't recognize.

"THEY'RE HERE FOR ME" thought Opal, "I have to get Amir to take me away!"

OPAL KNEW HER GIG WOULD be up and had to alert Amir somehow.

Flying Cuckoo

OPAL BEGAN TO FLAP her wings frantically trying to escape - this is much to Amir's surprise. He couldn't believe that Opal was flying.

"OPAL, YOU'RE FLYING!" laughed Amir.

THE CUCKOO LANDED NEAR the window near the fire escape.

"PLEASE GET ME OUT" thought Opal as she began to use her beak to tap on the glass.

AMIR HEADED OVER AND began to open the window. It was then that the SWAT team members began to bust down his door despite the various furniture blocking their path.

"EASY, DO NOT TRY ANYTHING crazy" said the SWAT team leader, "your family is just outside and they only want to help you."

"YOU ALL WANT TO TAKE ME AWAY FROM OPAL!" bellowed Amir.

AMIR THEN GRABBED THE cuckoo and opened the window, he then began to use the ladders on the fire escape to escape to the street level. The SWAT team couldn't believe how desperate Amir was to flee from them.

"WE HAVE TO GO BACK to the ground level now!" ordered the SWAT team leader.

THE SWAT TEAM MEMBERS soon rushed out with Officers Anna and Dylan following them.

Pursuing Amir

AMIR HAD THE FIRST start getting ahead on foot, though he felt he knew it wouldn't last.

"I HAVE TO GET YOU TO the park, you'll be safe there" said Amir.

THE PARK WAS THE ONE sure place Amir could figure out would be a safe place. Already he could hear sirens in the distance chasing after him. His family were also tailing the police in their family car while Arthur and Bachir took their own cars.

"I CAN'T BELIEVE OUR son is running away from us!" cried Saliha.

"IT FEELS SO AMAZING with this chase!" laughed Kamel.

SALIHA SOON SLAPS HER husband as he drives.

"THIS IS OUR SON WE'RE talking about" said Saliha.

"CAN'T I HAVE THE RIGHT to joke about it?" asked Kamel.

SALIHA SHOOK HER HEAD angrily at her husband. Tahar and Farida did their best trying to stay silent. The police and the SWAT team could see that Amir was heading towards the park where he found the bird - it made so much sense. As Amir arrived at the park first he was desperate trying to find a possible nest for Opal to stay in.

Searching for Shelter

AMIR RUSHED AROUND the park and headed towards the nearby lake. He felt compelled that it'd be safer there.

"I HAVE TO OUTRUN THEM!" cried Amir.

AMIR HID AROUND SOME trash cans with Opal in his hand.

"THANK YOU FOR RESCUING me" said Opal.

AMIR THOUGHT HE WAS imaging things - did the bird just speak to him? No that was silly thought Amir. The SWAT team and the police officers parked their vehicles along with the Laurent family and their friends. They were all worried for Amir's safety.

"PLEASE OFFICERS GO easy on my son this is his first time in trouble with the law" said Saliha.

"WE UNDERSTAND" SAID Officer Anna, "I think the bird is the problem."

TAHAR SMILED WITH JOY, he couldn't believe those in law enforcement were on his side. Though the police and SWAT teams didn't think the suspected cuckoo was demonic - Tahar still thought otherwise. Arthur and Bachir soon parked their cars and got out.

"YOUR BROTHER MUST NOT be far" said Arthur to Tahar and the rest of the Laurent family.

"DON'T WORRY, WE'LL find Amir" said Saliha, "and bring him home."

26

SALIHA WAS DETERMINE that Amir would calm down, but Amir wasn't about to go quietly.

Chapter Three

Amir Hiding in the Park

Hours ticked by, Amir felt he had been hiding in the park for days when it wasn't the fact. Opal smiled as the cuckoo knew her plan was working all along.

"NOW YOU CAN TAKE CARE of me and be with me forever!" cried Opal.

AMIR STILL SHOOK HIS head pretending he didn't hear her speak.

"DON'T WORRY LITTLE bird, I will make sure those men will not be taking you away from me" said Amir.

AMIR'S NAME WAS BEING called out by his family who were searching for him. Farida was getting closer to his location.

"AMIR, BROTHER, WHERE are you we are searching for you!" cried Farida.

FARIDA COULD TELL HER brother was near and felt compelled to find him first before the SWAT team members or Officers Anna and Dylan could.

"EVERYONE IS LOOKING for you!" cried Farida, "I miss you!"

THAT "I MISS YOU" CAUGHT Amir's attention as he peaked out from his hiding place among the bushes. There Farida was searching for her brother, desperate that he come home.

"THEY'RE SEARCHING FOR me" said Amir.

OPAL KNEW SHE HAD TO reveal her true intentions soon so she could fool Amir longer.

Fooling Amir

OPAL WAS PLEASED HOW long Amir managed to take care of her. She flapped her wings off of her pillow and landed near him.

"AMIR LAURENT, I AM the bird you have raised" said Opal.

AMIR SHOOK HIS HEAD again for a second time thinking he couldn't believe a bird was talking.

"BIRDS DON'T TALK, THAT'S silly" thought Amir.

"BUT I AM VERY MUCH real Amir, I have been watching you since the moment you picked my egg out of the wood pigeon's nest that my mother placed me there" said Opal.

AMIR COULDN'T BELIEVE it - a talking bird impossible! He was doing his best trying to put the two together regarding his older brother Tahar's superstitious beliefs on the bird in question before him.

"WAIT, MY BROTHER TAHAR was right about you?!" cried Amir.

OPAL NODDED.

"I NEED YOU TO TAKE care of me, do not let your fellow humans take me away" continued Opal.

OPAL CONTINUED TO PLAY up the deceit, hoping her human host would continue taking care of her. Amir agreed to her terms as he began to bow down and pray. The cuckoo couldn't believe her plans were coming together!

Distracting Farida

OPAL KNEW SHE HAD TO come up with a plan to prevent Farida from finding Amir.

"I WILL THROW MY VOICE over to the other bush nearby thinking that you are there instead" said Opal.

AMIR CLAPPED HIS HANDS with joy.

"YES, YES, DO THAT" said Amir.

OPAL SOON PREPARED to use her powers and soon threw her voice over to the bush near Farida.

"CHIRP, CHIRP, CHIRP!" bellowed Opal as she began the call in her bird language.

FARIDA TURNED AROUND thinking her brother was in the nearby bush. Officers Anna and Dylan soon arrived.

"MY BROTHER IS BEHIND this bush" said Farida.

THE TWO POLICE OFFICERS began to approach with caution using only batons this time as a self-defense tool. As they began to look through the bush - there was nothing there.

"ARE YOU IMAGING YOUR brother was behind here?" asked Officer Dylan.

"BUT, I COULD HAVE SWORN I heard the cry of that bird behind the bush" said Farida.

FARIDA WAS NO DOUBT disappointed in not finding her brother, she knew time was ticking away and the other members of the family along with their two more religious friends were having no luck either.

Search Party Regroups

THE SWAT TEAM MEMBERS along with the Laurent family, Arthur Boucher and Bachir Muhamed all gathered again around the center of the park. Amir was nowhere to be found.

"I AM WORRIED MY SON isn't coming home" said Saliha.

"YOUR SON IS AN ADULT, he should be able to take care of him" said a SWAT team member.

"CAN'T YOU USE YOUR night vision goggles to find my son in this park?" asked Kamel.

"THAT COULD TAKE THE entire evening" said the SWAT team leader.

"PLEASE, I AM BEGGING you to find my son" continued Saliha.

THE SWAT TEAM MEMBERS knew they were going to be camping in the park overnight trying to find Amir. Officers Anna and Dylan also decided to stay with the search party in terms of camping out.

"WE WILL STAY WITH ALL of you and see this through" said Officer Anna to the Laurent family, "you have our word."

SALIHA AND KAMEL CUDDLED together comforting each other in this time of need. Tahar felt guilty of being responsible for leading to his brother Amir's mental breakdown.

"I FEEL SO SHAMEFUL for all of this" sighed Tahar to Arthur and Bachir.

NEITHER RELIGIOUS MAN knew it was truly Tahar's fault and knew they had to calm him down.

Part Two

Chapter Four

Calming Tahar Down

Arthur and Bachir could tell that Tahar felt guilty of Amir's mental breakdown. How he managed to escape the apartment so fast.

"THERE, THERE TAHAR, it's not your fault" said Bachir.

"ABSOLUTELY IT ISN'T your fault" added Arthur, "you were trying to provide an intervention to your brother's issue with that bird that he was taking care of."

"YES, YOU WERE DOING the right thing" said Bachir.

"I AM UNSURE, I AM HAVING second thoughts of inviting both of you over" continued Tahar, "my brother would still be in his room taking care of the bird, and getting the bird rice. I ruined that chance for him."

"BUT PERHAPS YOU CAN make it up by finding him and apologizing to him" added Arthur.

BOTH RELIGIOUS MEN could get the feeling that would be the right mood. Tahar knew he would have to work hard with his sister Farida to find Amir. Farida was being comforted by Officers Anna and Dylan over failing to find Amir.

"I REALLY THOUGHT MY brother was behind that bush" said Farida.

"WELL, WHEN YOU'RE SEARCHING for a love one you think your love one is everywhere" added Officer Dylan.

FARIDA STILL FELT CONFIDENT her brother was somewhere in the park.

Getting Dark

IT WAS GETTING DARK in the park and Amir was doing his best trying to setup a campfire to keep himself warm. Opal was cozying up to the campfire with him.

"IT'S NICE TO FIND A human that will take care of me, I thought I would have fooled that wood pigeon if it were not for you" said Opal.

OPAL BEGAN TO PUT HER head on Amir like a cat would.

"I DON'T CARE IF THIS is all in my head, I will do my best to find food for you" said Amir.

AMIR DECIDED TO DIG for worms for Opal, it was the only source of food he could think of. As he dug with his bear hands, he found a few earthworms and grabbed them. He then took a rock and began to smash them into pieces making it easier for Opal to scarf them down.

"I DON'T HAVE A SPOON to feed you or that glove but I will have to use my hands" said Amir.

IT WAS GROSS AND DISGUSTING, but Amir had to do it as he showed the bird the mashed up worms.

Opal Enjoys a Meal

IT WASN'T THE SAME as rice or regular meal worms from the pet store. It was rather different taste eating mashed up worms from the wild. She began to eat them with her beak.

"SO GOOD, I WONDER IF I stayed in that wood pigeon's nest I would have had this but then I would have knocked out my siblings from the nest first!" laughed Opal.

AMIR DIDN'T SEEM TO care about Opal's dark intentions as he continued to feed her.

"MORE, MORE, I WANT more!" cried Opal as she flapped her wings.

AMIR WAS GETTING TIRED, but he knew Opal's needs were more important.

"DON'T WORRY, I WILL get more for you" said Amir.

AMIR DUG AGAIN WITH his bear hands and surely enough he found more worms. He took a few and crushed them with a rock. He then grabbed the mashed up worms and began to feed it to Opal.

"THERE YOU GOT OPAL" said Amir.

"THANK YOU, THANK YOU human!" laughed Opal with joy.

SHE CONTINUED TO EAT, she didn't know how much time they'd have in the park knowing the search party was around.

Searching in the Dark

TAHAR AND FARIDA WERE given extra flashlights by Officers Anna and Dylan. The four of them began to search the park together.

"IT'S SO DARK" SAID Farida.

"DON'T WORRY SISTER, we will find our brother and bring him home" said Tahar.

OFFICERS ANNA AND DYLAN separated with Officer Anna going with Farida and Officer Dylan going with Tahar.

"DON'T WORRY, WE WILL find your brother together" said Officer Dylan.

"YES, I CAN'T BELIEVE I feel so guilty of starting this mess" said Tahar.

"LIKE THOSE TWO RELIGIOUS folks said it's not your fault Amir made his choice to run with the bird" continued Officer Dylan.

"YES, I KNOW BUT STILL if I didn't bring over Arthur and Bachir we wouldn't be in this mess" added Tahar.

"THAT'S TRUE" SAID OFFICER Dylan.

TAHAR THEN NOTICED some holes around the park. They were dug by human hands.

"MY BROTHER MUST BE near, he must be digging holes to find worms for that dreaded bird" said Tahar.

"WELL HE COULDN'T HAVE gone that far, let's move, I will radio in Officer Anna" said Officer Dylan.

OFFICER DYLAN BEGAN to let Officer Anna know where they were.

Messed Up Amir

TAHAR AND OFFICER DYLAN could hear Amir's voice in the distance as they began to creep up behind a bush. Officer Dylan began to radio in Officer Anna.

"OFFICER ANNA BESSETTE, this is Officer Dylan Desmarais, we have located Amir Laurent" whispered Officer Dylan.

"WE MUST BE VERY QUIET no telling what my brother would do if he spotted us" said Tahar.

TAHAR WANTED TO MOVE with caution, he decided to turn off his flashlight and started to creep around. He could get the feeling his brother was close. As he began to sneak by, he could hear Amir talking to Opal, and then Opal speaking to him. Opal had a high feminine voice trying to coax him into taking care of her forever.

"I AM SO HAPPY I FOUND a human to take care of me instead of another bird" said Opal, "I felt the wood pigeon wouldn't be able to provide for me."

TAHAR WAS CAREFUL TO avoid any twigs on the park ground along with Officer Dylan who began to follow Tahar. Officer Anna and Farida soon arrived preparing to help the two men try to get Amir.

Chapter Five

Moving In

Tahar and Farida were moving in with Officers Anna and Dylan. They were careful not to make any sudden movements. The SWAT team were also prepared to join them in case if Amir got violent in any fashion.

"STANDING BY" WHISPERING the SWAT team leader.

FOR AMIR, HE COULD hear rustling in the distance and knew it had to be the search party. He was in panic mode unsure what to do next. Opal knew this was her chance to shine by revealing herself to him.

"PLEASE AMIR, YOU HAVE to listen to me" said Opal.

AMIR PAUSED IT COULDN'T be just his imagination running wild - the bird was speaking to him.

"LITTLE BIRDIE, HOW are you speaking to me?" asked Amir.

"BECAUSE YOU TOOK SUCH good care of me, I have learned your language" continued Opal.

OPAL KNEW HOW TO PLAY these clever tricks on Amir's mind. She could manipulate him to do whatever she wanted. But she felt since the SWAT team was on his trail, he would have to bail with her.

"YOU HAVE TO FIND SHELTER but not in the park" said Opal.

AMIR CONTINUED TO LISTEN to the cuckoo bird, unaware of her ill-intentions.

Amir on the Move

AMIR KNEW HE HAD TO pick up the pace and leave or he'll surely be spotted. He grabbed Opal and her pillow and began to make a run for it across the park.

"DON'T WORRY LITTLE birdie, I will find a safe place for you!" cried Amir.

OPAL WAS TRYING TO figure out what sort of shelter Amir should take her. The sewer was out of the question, she hated its smell and disgusting odor. She then noticed a greenhouse garden in the distance within the park.

"THAT PLACE WILL DO nicely" said Opal.

"YES LITTLE BIRDIE, whatever you say little birdie" said Amir.

AMIR TREKKED TOWARDS the greenhouse garden in the distance he could see it would provide enough protection, shelter and even food for the both of them. Amir began to inspect the lock and used a twig as a lock pick trying to open it.

"DON'T WORRY LITTLE birdie, I will get ourselves to safety" said Amir.

AMIR THEN MANAGED TO open the door with the twig as a lock pick, grabbed Opal and the pillow and headed inside the greenhouse garden. There he could see various fruit trees growing. It would be a lovely place for the both of them to stay.

Holding Up in the Greenhouse Garden

TAHAR, FARIDA AND OFFICERS Anna and Dylan missed Amir by a few minutes. They could see the greenhouse garden in the distance being the likely place of shelter that Amir and the suspected cuckoo had taken shelter.

"GREAT, I THINK OUR brother is inside there" said Tahar.

THE SWAT TEAM ALL PAUSED as they arrived on the scene. The SWAT team leader used his flashlight and shined right inside the greenhouse garden.

"THERE'S NO WAY WE CAN enter without a search warrant sorry" said the SWAT team leader.

"BUT YOU CAN JUST BREAK in" said Tahar.

"AGAINST THE LAW" SAID the SWAT team leader, "I am calling this off."

THE SWAT TEAM LEADER felt in the right not to proceed, that left it up to Officers Anna and Dylan to decide their next moves. Kamel along with Saliha, Bachir and Arthur arrived on the scene.

"A GREENHOUSE GARDEN, that shelter might make the most sense" said Arthur.

ARTHUR ALWAYS WANTED to venture inside the greenhouse garden, but couldn't since it was privately owned.

"WE WOULD HAVE TO CONTACT the owner and have Amir come out" said Saliha.

"WE'LL FIGURE OUT A way to get our son safely out" said Kamel.

TAHAR AND FARIDA KNEW their brother would be in deep trouble after this was all lover.

Enough Resources

WHILE AMIR'S FAMILY worried outside the greenhouse garden, Amir was having the time of his life gathering the various fruits from the trees for Opal. He was determine to make her happy and quite comfortable.

"DON'T WORRY LITTLE birdie, I will feed you these fruit it's not rice but it'd do" said Amir.

OPAL KNEW SHE HAD NO choice but to accept the fruit. It would take sometime before she could ever have rice again. Amir like before began to mash up some of the fruit. The oranges were the easier to peel and mash up while the apples were much harder. He was able to feed Opal the mashed up oranges with ease by using his hands.

"THERE YOU GO LITTLE birdie" said Amir.

OPAL SIGHED AS SHE began to use her beak to eat the mashed up oranges. It felt like a strange meal for her, but what other sort of choices she had? Amir could tell his family were still outside. They were doing their best trying to contact the owner of the greenhouse garden.

"THEY HAVEN'T GIVEN up" said Amir.

"YOU CAN STAY WITH ME inside here" said Opal.

OPAL WAS DOING HER best trying to discourage Amir from looking at his family.

Keeping Amir Away

OPAL, IN HER CUCKOO-like nature knew she had to keep Amir away from his family if she wanted to keep the human host. Unlike a usual bird host for a cuckoo, a human would be more difficult to convince. For Opal, it was unnatural for birds like her to speak to humans but in this instance it was an emergency.

"YOU HAVE TO UNDERSTAND your family want to give me up" said Opal.

"I DON'T WANT ANYTHING bad to happen to you little birdie" said Amir.

"I KNOW YOU WILL DO your best to protect me if I am taken away even fight for me" added Opal.

"YES, FIGHT, I AM A fighter for you Opal" said Amir.

OPAL LAUGHED IN HER mind knowing how easy it was to manipulate Amir. Amir would stoop to even fighting his own family if they got inside the greenhouse garden. Meanwhile, outside the greenhouse garden, Farida was doing her best trying to research who the owner was. She was desperate for answers since they really wanted their brother to come home safe and sound.

"ANY LUCK WHO OWNS THE greenhouse garden?" asked Saliha.

"I AM DOING MY BEST" said Farida.

FARIDA WAS DOING HER research on her cellphone.

Chapter Six

The Greenhouse Garden Owner

Farida finally found the greenhouse garden owner - Celia Marouk - a fellow French-Algerian who had a permit for the greenhouse garden for the city of Lyon. Farida began to call the number of her contact on her cellphone.

"HELLO?" ASKED CELIA as she picked it up in her apartment.

"THIS IS FARIDA LAURENT speaking" said Farida, "our brother Amir is inside your greenhouse garden. The police are with us and we'd like to get your permission to enter inside."

CELIA COULD TELL THIS was a serious matter, she got dressed and began to head out.

"DON'T WORRY, I WILL be heading towards the park immediately" said Celia.

CELIA SOON HEADED OUT of her apartment and it took her just a few minutes to arrive at the park. She gazed over at the greenhouse and could see Amir inside with what appeared to be a cuckoo.

"THAT'S A CUCKOO BIRD" said Celia.

"HA, TOLD YOU ALL IT was" laughed Tahar.

TAHAR FELT RELIEVED he wasn't the only one aside from Arthur over the cuckoo bird.

"LUCKY FOR YOU I CAN let ourselves in" said Celia.

EVERYONE HAD TO PROCEED with caution unsure what Amir would do.

Proceeding Inside

CELIA SOON ALLOWED everyone in, the Laurent family began to search for Amir along with Officers Anna and Dylan. Bachir and Arthur both agreed to stay behind in case if Amir tried to escape.

"WOW, WHAT AN INCREDIBLE place!" laughed Officer Dylan.

"I KNOW, ISN'T IT?" asked Celia.

CELIA WAS PLEASED TO have outsiders admire her garden she was growing inside the greenhouse. As they continued to search for Amir they could hear that Amir was speaking to the bird itself. Tahar decided to go first since he was more familiar with the "demonic" bird.

"THAT BIRD IS DEMONIC, I was right after all" laughed Tahar with confirmation.

FARIDA WAS EVEN PERPLEXED as she also joined her brother to observe Amir. He was talking to the bird.

"MAYBE HE JUST HAS A mental breakdown" said Farida.

"LOOK AT THE BIRD IT'S speaking back to him because it's a demon" said Tahar.

TAHAR AND FARIDA LISTENED carefully, even Kamel and Saliha were curious.

"BE CAREFUL" SAID SALIHA.

BOTH SIBLINGS KNEW they had to approach their brother with caution. Farida thought Amir was either having a mental breakdown, or under the influence of some substance. Tahar felt confident the bird was demonic.

Approaching Amir

SLOWLY BUT SURELY, both Tahar and Farida cautiously approached Amir. They could see he was very protective of his cuckoo - Opal. He didn't realize he was taking care of a cuckoo at all.

"HE IS SO UNAWARE OF what kind of bird it is" whispered Tahar.

TAHAR CONTINUED TO creep closer and closer along with Farida. Officers Anna and Dylan soon did the same. They could tell that Amir could go bonkers at any moment.

"JUST BE VERY CAREFUL" whispered Officer Dylan, "we're backing both of you."

TAHAR AND FARIDA NODDED as they moved forward. Amir was still unaware that they entered the greenhouse and neither was Opal aware.

"LITTLE BIRDIE, WE CAN stay here forever, you are right there's enough food that'd last us several months" said Amir.

"YES, THAT'S RIGHT AMIR you are a wonderful caretaker for me" said Opal.

OPAL SOON NOTICED TAHAR in the distance approaching, she began to flap her wings frantically.

"WHAT'S GOING ON GIRL?" asked Amir.

"INTRUDERS" WHISPERED Opal.

AMIR GLANCED OVER AND surely enough, he spotted Tahar and Farida. He was clearly spooked on how they could get inside the greenhouse unaware the owner allowed them in.

Amir Tries to Escape

AMIR DECIDED TO GRAB Opal and makes a run for it along with the pillow. Opal could see Tahar leading the chase.

"GET THAT DEMONIC BIRD!" bellowed Tahar.

AMIR COULDN'T BELIEVE that his own brother - Tahar thought the bird was demonic.

"YOU ARE NOT A DEMON, are you little birdie?" asked Amir.

OPAL SHOOK HER HEAD.

"THAT HUMAN IS CLEARLY crazy" remarked Opal.

TAHAR CONTINUED TO chase his brother, Amir decided to throw a few potted plants against him. Celia gasped at how the hard work she had done was just destroyed just like that.

"STOP THROWING MY PLANTS!" cried Celia.

OFFICERS ANNA AND DYLAN soon were able to catch up to Amir, Officer Dylan attempted to lunge at Amir in the hopes of tackling him, but Amir was able to slip right through.

"YOU'LL NEVER STOP ME FROM TAKING CARE OF OPAL!" cried Amir.

AMIR HOPED HE COULD find another exit in the greenhouse garden, he couldn't believe how everyone was after him.

"LEAVE ME AND MY OPAL ALONE!" cried Amir.

FARIDA SOON WAS ABLE to catch up to her brother. She knew she had to convince him to give up the bird and come home.

Chapter Seven

Amir's Destructive Behavior

Amir was running out of options what to do next, Opal knew she had to encourage his behavior to deteriorate even further.

"THROW THE POTTED PLANTS at them" whispered Opal.

AMIR COULDN'T RESIST hearing Opal out, he leaned over towards some potted plants that were around him and began to throw them at Tahar, Farida and Celia.

"MY PLANTS!" CRIED CELIA as she dodged a couple of them.

AMIR WAS TOO FOCUSED on protecting Opal to be worried about himself. Saliha and Kamel could see how much of a mental breakdown their son Amir was having. Officers Anna and Dylan did their best trying to calm him down.

"PLEASE, YOU HAVE TO remain calm, we are not here to hurt you" said Officer Anna.

OFFICER DYLAN WAS GETTING ready his baton to help Farida and Tahar.

"ENOUGH OF THIS!" CRIED Officer Dylan.

OFFICER DYLAN STEPPED in between the Laurent siblings, Amir was increasingly frustrated with not being able to flee the greenhouse.

"I HAVE EVERY RIGHT to protect Opal!" bellowed Amir.

"THAT BIRD IS THE REASON why you have broken down" continued Officer Dylan.

THE OFFICER BEGAN TO approach Amir with caution, Officer Anna knew Amir could lunge at him at any moment.

Lunging at Officer Dylan

IT WAS AMIR'S MISTAKE for listening to Opal to attack anyone that came after him. Opal managed to hide during the commotion around some plants.

"I WILL NOT LET YOU take me from Opal!" cried Amir.

AMIR WAS ON TOP OF Officer Dylan, the officer couldn't reach his taser.

"GET MY TASER!" CRIED Officer Dylan to Tahar and Farida.

TAHAR SOON GRABBED the taser from Officer Dylan's pocket. He hated to do this to his own brother, but Amir was acting out too much.

"I AM SORRY TO DO THIS to you brother, forgive me!" cried Tahar.

TAHAR AIMED THE TASER carefully, hoping not to miss Amir. He closed his eyes and soon fired the taser - ZAP! The taser managed to zap Amir as the wires attached to his back. The shock jolted Amir causing him to tumble backwards. Opal could see the human she had tricked fall quite hard on the ground.

"AMIR!" CRIED OPAL.

THE CUCKOO KNEW SHE would be surely caught if she ran to his side. Farida soon rushed over with Officer Anna to make sure Amir was okay. Amir was still breaching, despite the shock from the taser.

Taking Amir Out

AMIR SOON WAS PICKED up by both Farida and Officer Anna, they soon were followed by Tahar, Officer Dylan and Celia. Saliha, Kamel, Arthur and Bachir were outside waiting for them.

"AMIR!" CRIED SALIHA with joy.

SALIHA COULD SEE AMIR was regaining consciousness from the taser.

"UH, WHAT HAPPENED?" asked Amir.

"YOU TRIED TO ASSAULT me, but I think you were under some sort of influence" said Officer Dylan.

"AN INFLUENCE FROM A demonic bird" added Tahar.

OFFICERS DYLAN AND Anna knew the Laurent family would have sometime to recover from this episode. But the suspected cuckoo was still missing - Opal was still within the greenhouse. She was eager to eventually try to slip through to find Amir.

"DON'T WORRY AMIR, I will find you" said Opal as she was behind the greenhouse glass window.

THE CUCKOO KNEW SHE had to get out, though there was plenty of food for her to eat on her own. For the Laurents, they soon left the park carrying Amir home. Saliha felt relieved that the entire ordeal was over and so was Kamel.

"WE SHOULD PROBABLY have our son rest for a few days" added Kamel.

"YES, THAT'S A GOOD idea" replied Saliha.

AS THE LAURENT FAMILY soon arrived home, Amir was taken back to his room.

Opal's Mind Games

AMIR WAS PLACED IN his bed by Tahar and Farida, they then headed out back to their usual activities.

"YOU THINK OUR BROTHER will be okay?" asked Farida.

"I AM SURE, NOW THE crazy demon bird is gone" said Tahar.

"WHY DO YOU KEEP ON saying the bird was a demon?" asked Farida, "it's just a bird that Amir got too worked up about."

"THERE ARE CERTAIN THINGS in the world that we do not understand" continued Tahar, "I suspect the demon bird could try to make his or her way back to our apartment."

FARIDA THOUGHT THAT was a silly idea that her older brother was thinking. But Tahar was right to think that way. When Celia decided to head back to her greenhouse to clean up the mess, she opened the door just ajar. It was just enough for Opal to find her way out.

"I HAVE TO AVOID ANY predators on my way to Amir's place" said Opal.

OPAL WASN'T FINISHED yet, she was determine to get home and find her human host. It was an easy trek from the park, but the alleyway was another story.

Part Three

Chapter Eight

Avoiding Stray Cats

Opal managed to find herself in a familiar alleyway setting that was just near the apartment complex where the Laurent family lived. Opal could see a few cats searching the trash for anything to eat. The cats were mostly tabby cats, either orange or black searching the trash.

"MEOW, MEOW" REMARKED an orange tabby as it began to search the trash.

THEN THE EARS OF A black tabby cat perked up and noticed Opal in the distance.

"MEOW!" CRIED THE BLACK tabby cat.

THE ALLEYWAY CATS COULD see the bird as clear as day - dinner they all thought! Opal knew she better make a run for it. She flew up on the fire escape ladder, she would be hoping to lose the alleyway cats. However at least one orange and black tabby cat began to follow her.

"THOSE CATS WON'T LEAVE me alone, I have to get Amir's attention!" cried Opal in her head.

THE CUCKOO DID HER best to flew up each of the flights of the fire escape ladder. She could get the feeling she was getting closer and closer to Amir's room. But the alleyway cats were on her tail.

Escape Ladder Chase!

IT FELT AS IF IT WERE something out of a retro cartoon - a bird trying to escape some hungry alleyway cats! The orange and black tabby cats did their best trying to climb up on the escape ladder.

"MEOW!" CRIED THE ORANGE tabby.

"MEOW!" CRIED THE BLACK tabby.

OPAL COULD TELL THEY were pretty hungry and determined to get her. She knew she was just a few floors away before reaching Amir's.

"I JUST HAVE TO KEEP on trying!" cried Opal to herself in her head.

SHE CONTINUED TO CLIMB, and climb and climb but so did the two alleyway cats! The two stray cats were determined to get their meal. But Opal soon managed to make her way to the familiar fire escape ladder that Amir had climbed out of earlier. This had to be the right fire escape ladder!

"I HOPE I CAN GET HIS attention" said Opal.

OPAL THEN HOPPED RIGHT onto the edge of a window and noticed Amir was in his bed resting from his ordeal. She could see how bruised up he was with the fight with Officer Dylan. She then began to tap on the glass with her beak trying to get his attention.

The Tapping Sound

TAP, TAP, TAP, OPAL began to use her beak to tap on the glass window. It sure got Amir's attention as he slowly began to open his eyes.

"W-W-WHO'S THERE?" ASKED Amir.

AMIR COULD SEE IT WAS Opal at the window!

"OPAL, YOU FOUND YOUR WAY HOME!" cried Amir with joy.

AMIR SOON OPENED UP the window and grabbed Opal just in the nick of time before the two alleyway cats could get her. No doubt the two cats were disappointed and soon began to make their way down the fire escape ladder system. Amir hugged Opal in his arm so happy to see the birdie before him.

"I WILL NEVER LET YOU OUT OF MY SIGHT, NO ONE CAN TAKE YOU AWAY FROM ME!" laughed Amir.

"YES HUMAN, YOU ARE right, no one can take me away from you EVER!" laughed Opal.

THE LAUGH FROM THE cuckoo almost sounded sinister, but Amir didn't seem to care too much. He got Opal a new pillow for her nest and planted her right there.

"THERE YOU GO LITTLE birdie, I will go fetch you more rice from the Chinese restaurant" said Amir.

OPAL, IF SHE COULD smile would have a sinister grin on her face.

Cheerful Amir

AMIR SOON HEADED OUT from his room, he had cleaned himself up from the bruises from the fight he had with Officer Dylan. Farida was surprised to see her brother doing so well.

"BROTHER, YOU'RE OKAY!" laughed Farida.

FARIDA WAS ABOUT TO hug him, when Amir refused the hug.

"I AM SORRY SISTER, but I have to get rice for Opal, she returned to me!" laughed Amir.

FARIDA WAS SPOOKED she could have sworn Amir had lost Opal during the commotion at the greenhouse. As she peaked through underneath the floor, Opal soon peaked right back at her starling Farida.

"THE BIRD, IT'S BACK!" cried Farida.

FARIDA NEARLY TUMBLED with the surprise jump scare by the cuckoo. She knew Tahar had to be right after all with the "demon" bird. She knew she had to get further answers from him. She headed over to the main living room area to find Tahar was doing his usual activities - watching his shows through streaming services.

"YES SISTER?" ASKED Tahar as he turned to her.

"THE BIRD, IT'S BACK" said Farida, "Amir was a bit too happy when he emerged from his room."

"I WAS AFRAID THIS WAS going to happen" sighed Tahar.

TAHAR PAUSED HIS STREAMING service shows to take a look for himself.

Chapter Nine

Opal and Tahar

Tahar headed over to the hallway and towards Amir's room. Farida pointed at the door.

"I SAW HIM AS I PEAKED through underneath the door" said Farida.

"LET ME SEE IF WHAT you are saying is true" said Tarah.

TARAH SOON DID THE same, he peaked his head underneath the door and surely enough Opal peaked right back at him.

"HELLO PESKY HUMAN" said Opal.

TAHAR WAS SPOOKED OVER the fact the bird spoke to him!

"THE BIRD, IT SPEAKS!" cried Tahar, "It must have been giving Amir commands during the commotion we had at the park!"

FARIDA GASPED AT THE shock, though she was always the one who tried to be more logical. This was beyond her own knowledge!

"THERE HAS TO BE SOMEONE who could help us!" cried Farida.

"I TRIED ARTHUR, BUT it seems the bird managed to get the better of me" said Tahar, "even Bachir won't be any good."

TAHAR KNEW HE WOULD have to do some research to find an expert that would help him capture a pesky cuckoo bird. He couldn't just find anyone to do it, this individual would have to be known to hunt the most unusual creatures.

Getting an Expert

TAHAR AND FARIDA LOOKED at their cellphones for any possible experts. One name stood out from all of them - Diego Fortescue a known animal trapper who before the pandemic was renown to search the world for rare animals to capture. Tahar shrugged and felt he should take a chance with him.

"HELLO, IS THIS DIEGO Fortescue the World's Greatest Animal Trapper?" asked Tahar.

"YES, THIS IS HE?" REPLIED Diego, "Who is speaking?"

"I AM TAHAR LAURENT and my sister Farida, we have both been dealing with a pesky cuckoo bird who has been influencing our brother Amir" continued Tahar.

DIEGO HAD HEARD OF Amir's report from various news sources and knew this was a desperate move on the part of Amir's siblings.

"I WILL BE RIGHT OVER there, just give me a day and I will be there early in the morning" said Diego.

TAHAR KNEW HE HAD TO keep this a secret or Amir would surely run away with Opal again. Neither of them were interested in repeating that episode. For Amir, he was too busy getting rice from the local Chinese restaurant. The host was surprised that Amir was still willing to take care of the bird despite the commotion caused at the park.

Concerned for Amir

NO DOUBT THE REST OF the neighborhood had heard of the incident between him, his family and the bird he was trying to take care of. They all could see signs that Amir was breaking down mentally. The host of the Chinese restaurant didn't want to say too much.

"DON'T WORRY SIR, YOUR usual order of rice will be out shortly" said the host.

THE HOST HAD GAZED at videos of the report on social media through his cellphone. Even if some of the language was a cross between French and Chinese, he could understand what the reporters were saying.

"THE LAURENT FAMILY has been facing a crisis over Amir Laurent escaping from what appears to be a mere bird" said a female reporter, "it's unknown of what species of bird that would drive a man like that to go insane, but from remarks from his brother Tahar he stated the bird was possessed by a demon."

THE HOST LAUGHED AT Tahar's superstitious beliefs, unaware of how serious the matter was. Opal was manipulating Amir, but wasn't a demon, she was just a cuckoo who had become sentient.

Amir Heads Back

THE RICE ORDER WAS soon finished, and the host soon hands it over to Amir.

"HERE YOU GO, AND COME again" said the host.

AMIR NODDED AND SOON took off with the rice in the typical Chinese takeout. Amir continued to trek back to his apartment. Officers Anna Bessette and Dylan Desmarais were in their car and noticed Amir. He was too happy since the incident from the park.

"STRANGE, SOMEONE WHO would go through such an experience like that would stay inside for a couple of days" said Officer Dylan.

"WE SHOULD JUST KEEP a tab on him in case if something pops up" added Officer Anna.

BOTH POLICE OFFICERS were just concern for public safety, knowing Amir's breakdown at the greenhouse. They slowly began to follow him back to his apartment but at a very slow speed not to draw too much attention. Amir didn't seem to be bothered, he was too focused on taking care of Opal.

"I CAN'T BELIEVE OPAL returned to me!" laughed Amir with so much joy.

THE POLICE OFFICERS were surprised by his remarks - the bird returned to him, but how they both thought?

Chapter Ten

Keeping an Eye on Amir

Officers Anna and Dylan continued to follow Amir slowly in their police car. Amir was too cheerful to wonder who was following him.

"I CAN'T BELIEVE OPAL is back with me, I am so happy!" laughed Amir.

AMIR DANCED IN THE street which brought amusement to anyone who was out trying to do their typical chores.

"GLAD TO SEE YOU ARE happy" said a man on the street.

"YES, I AM SIR" SAID Amir.

AMIR SWUNG AROUND A traffic signal as if it were a typical lamp post. He was overjoy with happiness. He then crossed a street and the two cops continued to follow him.

"JUST TAKE NOTES ON his behavior" whispered Officer Anna.

OFFICER DYLAN NODDED, he had written down a few other notes before examining Amir's behavior. Though Amir wasn't dangerous at this stage, anything could change for the worse. Since they did after all see him escape from his own apartment complex. Amir eventually made it to the front entrance of the apartment complex.

"I AM GOING TO GET OUR supervisor to approve us having a stake out here" said Officer Anna.

AS OFFICER ANNA SEND her information to their supervisor, Amir was heading up on the elevator to the floor his family lived on.

Waiting on Amir

SALIHA HAD FINISHED making her meal for the family and paced out the plates. Kamel and Tarah were the first ones to sit down for their meals. Farida soon came in.

"WE'RE STILL WAITING on Amir" sighed Saliha.

FARIDA COULD TELL IT was because Opal had returned, that Amir was taking so long. Surely enough, Amir emerged through the front door.

"GREETINGS FAMILY, ONE moment while I feed my bird Opal" laughed Amir with joy.

AMIR SOON WHISTLED as he strolled off to his room. Tarah and Farida knew they had to tell their parents over hiring Diego Fortescue - the animal trapper.

"WE HAVE TO TELL THEM" whispered Tahar.

"TELL US WHAT DEAR?" asked Saliha.

"WE HIRED AN ANIMAL trapper, but it's because of that bird returning" whispered Farida.

"WELL COUNT US IN" CONTINUED Kamel, "I approve that you are taking action against that blasted bird that has divided us."

"YES, HOW MUCH WOULD it cost?" asked Saliha.

"HE DIDN'T SAY, BUT he would be coming over in a few days" said Farida.

ALL MEMBERS AT THE table soon stopped as soon as Amir sat down at his seat.

Not Giving Amir Any Hints

AMIR SAT DOWN AT HIS seat, ready to eat his meal.

"SO WHAT'S EVERYONE talking about, is about Opal returning?" asked Amir.

"UH, YES, YES IT SON we are so happy for you" said Kamel.

KAMEL WAS DOING HIS best trying to cover for Farida and Tarah.

"YES BROTHER, WE ARE very happy to see that you are happy" laughed Tarah.

"AW, THAT'S SO SWEET of you all" said Amir.

AMIR THEN HAD A GREAT idea in his head - why not show Opal around town?

"I GOT AN IDEA, I WAS thinking of maybe showing Opal around town" continued Amir as he began to eat his dinner.

THE FAMILY MEMBERS at the table at first didn't want to say anything, knowing the last time Opal was in public. Farida especially, when the bird was nearly identified as a cuckoo by those in her online session.

"UH, THAT'S A GREAT idea she'll get some exercise by doing it" said Farida.

FARIDA WAS NERVOUS, she couldn't believe she was agreeing with her brother Tarah that the suspected cuckoo bird known as Opal was bad news! Saliha and Kamel were agreeing with Tarah too.

Taking Opal Out

AFTER EVERYONE FINISHED the meal and went to bed, the following morning, Amir was up and ready. He brushed his teeth and got dressed. He checked on Opal.

"I WILL FEED YOU, LITTLE birdie, then we can take a stroll outside together" laughed Amir.

OPAL KNEW THIS WAS her chance to continue to manipulate Amir in public. She always wanted to show off her "powers" to the rest of the humans. Though the greenhouse fight was a separate episode of that display.

"IT SOUNDS LIKE A LOVELY idea" said Opal.

AMIR CHUCKLED AS HE could have sworn he heard her speak again. He brushed it off as he headed towards the kitchen to get some leftover rice. Amir soon headed towards the kitchen, he was given permission by his mother to take the leftover rice for the bird.

"GOOD THING I GOT PERMISSION this time" said Amir.

AMIR TOOK THE RICE and soon headed back to his room and fed Opal. Opal enjoyed that meal, for Amir he grabbed a small snack to go as his breakfast. He wasn't going to eat that much as he wanted to show Opal the world!

Epilogue

Sleeping Officers

While Amir was heading down from the floor he lived on, in his apartment complex; Officers Anna and Dylan were still fast asleep in their cop car. Officer Anna was the first one to wake up and began to shake her partner to get up.

"HE'S HEADING OUT" WHISPERED Officer Anna.

OFFICER DYLAN COULD see Amir emerge from the apartment.

"SHOULD WE FOLLOW HIM?" whispered Officer Dylan.

"YES, BUT SLOWLY" REPLIED Officer Anna.

OFFICER ANNA WAS AT the wheel and soon began to drive the police car at a slow speed. They didn't want to draw attention. They could see that Amir had brought out the bird, and Amir was going live with his cellphone on social media. He had his mask off as a way for the audience to see his face.

"HELLO EVERYONE, I WOULD all like you to meet Opal, my little birdie!" laughed Amir.

OPAL WANTED TO SHY away from the phone, knowing the audience could try to identify her. People were already making comments all over the world on his cellphone on social media.

"WHAT A STRANGE BIRD you have" remarked a woman user.

"YES, VERY STRANGE" added a second woman user.

AMIR CONTINUED TO STROLL on the street heading towards the park.

Amir at the Park

AMIR DECIDED TO VISIT the place where he had found Opal.

"IT'S BEEN QUITE SOMETIME since I found you in your nest" said Amir.

OPAL GAZED UP AT WHERE her nest once was - it was gone. The wood pigeons were all grown up and had flown away.

"SO MUCH HAS CHANGED" thought Opal to herself.

OPAL KNEW SHE HAD TO eventually be on her own, like a typical cuckoo would. However, she knew she'd have to stick around just one more time to cause trouble for Amir. Officers Anna and Dylan could see how close Opal was to Amir.

"HE BROUGHT THE BIRD with him" whispered Officer Dylan.

THE TWO OFFICERS CONTINUED to observe from their police car, not making any sudden moves. They were unsure what Amir would do next, for Amir he decided to sit by the tree with Opal.

"I AM SO HAPPY THAT we are together, we can finally spend so much time now" said Amir.

ALL AMIR WAS DOING was sitting by the tree and nothing more. The two officers sighed for the time being but knew they had to keep a watchful eye on him.

Diego Examines Opal

AMIR WAS A FOOL FOR live streaming himself and Opal on social media. Among those who caught the attention was Diego Fortescue the animal trapper that Farida and Tarah had hired. Diego wanted to get a closer look to see if this was the bird that Farida and Tarah were both speaking about.

"YEP, THAT LOOKS LIKE a cuckoo alright" said Diego as he examined the footage of the live stream.

DIEGO WAS PERPLEXED on how a cuckoo could have control over a single human being. It was so unnatural for an animal to have such control. Almost if it were a somewhat supernatural hold on Amir Laurent. He knew he would have to make his move very soon on the bird.

"NOW IS THE TIME TO examine my foe before I strike at it" laughed Diego.

DIEGO CONTINUED TO examine the live stream footage. Would Diego succeed in capturing Opal and forcing her to leave Amir? Would the Laurent family find peace after all of this? Find out in the next exciting book!

Don't miss out!

Visit the website below and you can sign up to receive emails whenever Maxwell Hoffman publishes a new book. There's no charge and no obligation.

https://books2read.com/r/B-A-JVYOC-GNFIF

BOOKS2READ

Connecting independent readers to independent writers.

Did you love *Amir Laurent: Fowl Play a Cuckoo Book 2 Greenhouse Fight*? Then you should read *Amir Laurent: Fowl Play A Cuckoo Tale Book 1 Opal's Deception*[1] by Maxwell Hoffman!

It is just the year after the pandemic and Amir Laurent has decided to take a walk in the park. Little does he realize he is about to come to face to face with the notorious cuckoo bird. However, he thinks the egg in the wood pigeon nest is just a mere wood pigeon egg and decides to take it home much against the advice of everyone around him.

Would Amir be able to take care of his bird named Opal? What secrets is Opal hiding from him that she doesn't want him to know? Or would his brother Tahar figure it out? Find out in this exciting tale.

Read more at https://www.instagram.com/vader7800/.

---

1. https://books2read.com/u/bMqNvG

2. https://books2read.com/u/bMqNvG

About the Author

I graduated from California State University with a BA in History. I am fond of historical fiction, science fiction, fantasy, and horror.
   Read more at https://www.instagram.com/vader7800/.

About the Publisher

I graduated from California State University of Northridge with a BA in History. I am fond of fantasy, science fiction, historical fiction and horror.

Read more at https://www.instagram.com/vader7800/.

Milton Keynes UK
Ingram Content Group UK Ltd.
UKHW030905011224
451693UK00001B/81